Lucy & Tom's 1.2.3.

SHIRLEY HUGHES

LONDON
VICTOR GOLLANCZ LTD
1991

80 · 79 · 78 · 77 · 76 · 75 · 74 · 73 · 72 · 71 · 70 · 69 · 68 · 67 · 66 · 65 · 64 · 63 · 62 · 61 · 60 · 59 · 58 · 57 · 56 · 55 · 54 · 53

52 · 51 · 50 · 49 · 48 · 47 · 46 · 45 · 44 · 43 · 42 · 41 · 40 · 39 · 38 · 37 · 36 · 35 · 34 · 33 · 32 · 31

100 · 99 · 98 · 97 · 96 · 95 · 94 · 93 · 92 · 91 · 90 · 89 · 88 · 87 · 86 · 85 · 84 · 83 · 82 · 81

First published in Great Britain May 1987
by Victor Gollancz Ltd,
14 Henrietta Street, London WC2E 8QJ
Second impression May 1991

British Library Cataloguing in Publication Data
Hughes, Shirley
  Lucy and Tom's 1.2.3.
  1. Numeration—Juvenile literature
  513′.5   QA141.3

  ISBN 0-575-03889-6

Printed in Hong Kong by Imago Publishing Ltd

One morning, very early…
one little girl called Lucy fast asleep in bed;
one tousled head cuddled down on the pillow,
one pink nose,
one mouth, a little bit open,
and one very special teddy tucked in beside her.

Lucy's little brother Tom is the first to wake up.
He opens both his eyes wide, jumps out of bed
and tugs at Lucy's quilt. Now there are two children,
wide awake and ready for another day.

It isn't time to get dressed yet but Tom puts on
some woolly socks to keep his toes warm. One is
blue and the other is striped. Not a proper pair,
but never mind.

Lucy's looking for something. She's lost one of
her slippers. Wherever is it? Good, here it is,
under the bed.

Lucy tips all her plastic animals out of their box
and she and Tom make them march across the
floor, two by two.

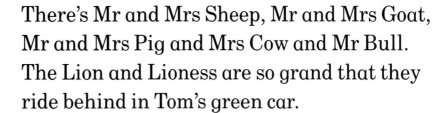 There's Mr and Mrs Sheep, Mr and Mrs Goat, Mr and Mrs Pig and Mrs Cow and Mr Bull. The Lion and Lioness are so grand that they ride behind in Tom's green car.

Tom builds up his bricks to make an arch for them all to go under.

Now Dad puts his head round the door and tells
them to come downstairs in their dressing-gowns.
Mum is having a little extra sleep this morning
so there are only three people for breakfast.

Lucy can lay the table: three mugs, three bowls,
three plates and three spoons. Just one knife
for Dad and a little spoon for him to stir his coffee.

Tom watches Dad cut the bread to make toast.
The toaster takes two slices of bread at a time,
so first they make two slices, one each for Lucy and Tom,
then two for Dad. When they are done Tom
arranges all four slices carefully in the toast-rack
and puts them on the table.

Today is Saturday.
No school this morning!
Lucy's clothes are on
the chair in Mum and
Dad's bedroom:
a vest and pants,
a pair of red socks,
a T-shirt with stripes
(first a red stripe,
then a blue one,
then a green),
a skirt and, last of all,
a pair of navy-blue shoes
with red laces.
Lucy can put them all on
by herself, all except for
tying the laces, that is.

Tom can put on his pants, one leg into each hole.
But he needs a bit of help with his sweater. Which
is the way out? It's all dark inside! At last he
finds both the arm-holes and then out pops his head.

As soon as they are dressed Lucy and Tom
go to see how Mopsa the cat is getting on.
A very exciting thing happened a few weeks ago.
Mopsa had kittens! She and her family are
living in a box in the corner of the kitchen.
It's very cosy inside with a bit of Lucy's old
woolly blanket for a bed.

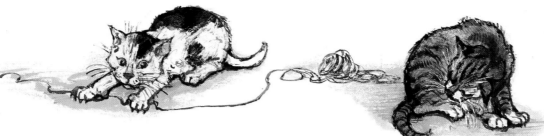

While Mopsa has her breakfast
the kittens come out to play
on the kitchen floor. There are
five of them, but only two are
tabby cats like Mopsa.

They have tiny claws, as many
on each paw as Lucy and Tom
have fingers on one hand, and
they're very sharp too!

Mum says that when the kittens are bigger they'll
be able to keep one and find good homes
for the other four. Lucy and Tom want
to keep them ALL! But six cats are rather
too many for one family.

It's time to go shopping. While Mum and Dad
search about for shopping bags and money,
Lucy and Tom are all ready and waiting
at the gate.

Out in the street there are
lots of things to count. There's
the windows in the house opposite,

the birds sitting on
the telephone wires,

people on the crossing,

and lampposts as far as the corner.

Paving stones are difficult.
They seem to go on for ever!

Number 5   Number 7   Number 9

Lucy and Tom's house is
Number 7. Next door on
one side is Number 9
and on the other is Number 5.
Number 4 , Number 6 and
Number 8 are across the
street. What a funny way
to count! But the postman
must get used to it.

Lucy knows that if she and Tom have four sweets,
or six or eight or even ten, they can share them
out equally. But if they have five or seven or
nine sweets they have to cut one of them in half or
else somebody is sure to be cross.
Luckily, today there's no trouble.

At last they are all off to the shops. At the super-
market there are a huge number of things to buy,
rows and rows of them. Tom rides on the trolley and
helps Mum to choose. They take packets and tins
off the shelves and Mum checks them off her
shopping list. Sometimes they come in ones, sometimes
in fours or sixes or even tens and twelves.

Lucy helps Dad to get the fruit and vegetables.
They put them into plastic bags and weigh them
on the scales. Let's see now . . . carrots, onions,
tomatoes, oranges; a pound of apples in one bag (only four
because they're quite heavy) and a pound of spinach
leaves in another (lots because they're much lighter).

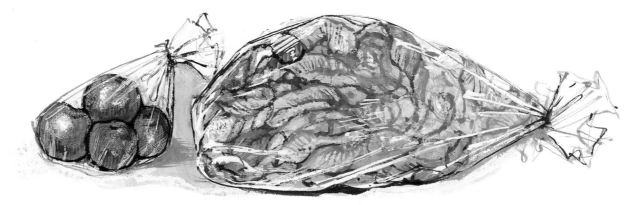

Last of all they buy a big box of chocolates for Granny because it's her birthday today. Also a tube of tiny little sweets, all different colours to decorate her cake. They're called Hundreds and Thousands. There are far too many to count.

Now for the check-out. Everyone stands in line waiting to pay. Dad packs all the things into shopping bags while Mum pays and the lady gives her the change.

On the way home they stop by a flower stall to buy
a bunch of flowers to take to Granny's birthday
tea-party that afternoon. Lucy and Tom help to
choose the colours, six bright red ones and five
creamy white, with some pretty green stuff to
go with them. Won't Granny be pleased?

Home again, Lucy and Tom go into
the back garden to play while Mum
and Dad unpack the shopping. Lucy
decides she will give her two old dolls
a bath in the big washing-up bowl.
It's too heavy to carry out when it's
full of water so Mum gives Lucy a
jug and says that she can fill up
the bath herself from the outside tap.
Lucy has to make a lot of rather drippy
journeys to and fro before it's ready.

Now in go the dolls for a good wash. Little Sophie
floats on the surface, bobbing about with her arms
and legs in the air. Poor Sarah has a hole in her
back. She soon fills up with water and sinks to
the bottom. Lucy has to rescue her and wrap her up
in a bit of towel in case she catches cold.

Tom's making a see-saw. He plays the game of putting different toys on it to see which one goes up in the air and which hits the ground.

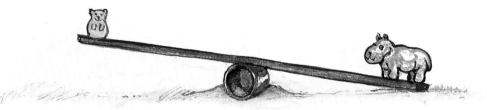

Sometimes you can get them to balance so that they're both up in the air at the same time.

When he gets tired of this Lucy helps him to make
a road for the cars to go along. Then Tom makes his
see-saw into a ramp. The cars go shooting down.
They have a race to see which car shoots
off furthest at the bottom. The big green
car wins. Then it's time for lunch.

After lunch Mum and Dad want to sit down for
a while before it's time to go to Granny and Grandpa's.
Mum gives Tom and Lucy a piece of paper each
to make birthday cards.

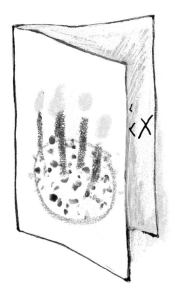

Tom folds his paper in half, like this. On the front he draws a picture of a big birthday cake with candles and lots of coloured dots all over it (those are the Hundreds and Thousands). Inside he writes his name and puts ten kisses.

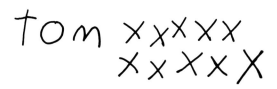

TOM XXXXX
XXXXX

Lucy folds her paper in half and then in half again. It looks smaller than Tom's. There's just room on the front to draw a picture of a bunch of flowers. But when you open it up, the back looks like this:

At last it's time to go to Granny's tea-party.
Granny is sixty today. She's very pleased with
her flowers and chocolates, and with Lucy and
Tom's cards which she puts on the mantelpiece
for everyone to see.

There's a very special tea with sandwiches,
biscuits, fancy pastries and a lovely big birthday
cake.

Granny says that she can't possibly blow
out her candles all by herself so Lucy and
Tom have to help her.

One, two, three, BLOW!
Happy Birthday, Granny!
Well done, Lucy and Tom!